D0532055

Moua, Doua, 1987-
Today is different /
[2022]
33305252173194
ca   05/20/22

TODAY IS DIFFERENT

DOUA MOUA

ILLUSTRATED BY **KIM HOLT**

SWEEP AWAY

Carolrhoda Books
Minneapolis

Every morning I eat fried eggs and warm rice with ice for breakfast with my parents and my brother, Tou . . .

BUT NOT TODAY.

Today everyone is distracted.

"What's happening?" I ask my mom.

"Don't worry, Mai," she tells me. "It doesn't have anything to do with you."

Every day my friend Kiara's father drops her off
at the bus stop . . .

BUT NOT TODAY.

"You coming with us, Mai?" asks the driver.

Every day Kiara and I share
our lunches together . . .

BUT NOT TODAY.

Every day Kiara and I play rocks during recess . . .

BUT NOT TODAY.

Today, Kiara is nowhere to be found.

During cleanup time, Mrs. Everitt walks by my desk.

"Where is Kiara?" I ask.

The bell rings before Mrs. Everitt can answer.

Today on the bus ride home from school, I see something
I've never seen before.

"What are all those people doing?" I ask.

I can see the bus driver's eyes in the rearview mirror,
but he doesn't say anything.

Every day Kiara and I skip home together . . .
BUT NOT TODAY.

The man who pushes his dog in a stroller is not out today either.

TODAY IS DIFFERENT.

Every day my mom meets me in the front yard,
but today she walks down the sidewalk to meet me.

"What are Dad and Tou doing?" I ask.

"We don't know what's going to happen,
so Dad and Tou are protecting the
house," Mom says. "Come
inside. We need to talk."

It's hard to hear the words coming out of my mother's mouth. What she says doesn't make any sense.

Why would the police hurt a man because he's Black?

"If we all stay home, we will be safe," Mom tells me. "Now go to your room."

Out of frustration, I dump out the colored pencils and stomp up to my room.

A moment later, Tou walks into my room.

He hands me my pencils.

"Tou, we're Hmong, so we're not Black
and we're not white, right?" I ask him.

He smiles at me. "We are Green."

"We are not Green," I say.

"Well, we speak in the Green dialect. In the Hmong culture, there are Black Hmong, White Hmong, Green Hmong, Striped Hmong, and many more. And all of us are Asian," Tou explains. "Just like your colored pencils. They come in different colors, but they are all pencils."

"I have an idea," Tou tells me. "Do you think you can help me make a sign?"

Tou always has a plan, so I shout, "Yes!"

"Shhhh," says Tou. "Don't let Mom and Dad hear us."

Tou leaves my room and then comes back with poster board and the broom from my witch costume I wore for Halloween.

"How do you spell *sweep*?" Tou asks.

"*S-W-E-E-P.*"

"How do you spell *away*?" he asks.

"That's an easy one . . . *A-W-A-Y,*" I say.

We use my colored pencils to write on the poster board in big letters.

"How do you spell
injustice?" Tou asks.

I shrug.

"What does Mom always put
in your warm rice?" he asks.

"In? Just ice . . ."

"That's it!" he says.

We tape the poster to the broom and then tiptoe to the front door.

I can hear Mom and Dad in the kitchen. "When are we going to talk to Mai about the world?" asks my dad.

"She's too young to understand," my mom says. "You are a father. You should want to protect her."

Instead of sneaking out, I march into the kitchen.

"Here, take this pencil and try to bend it," I tell my mom.

It breaks.

"Now try again," I say.

This time, I give her all the colored pencils.

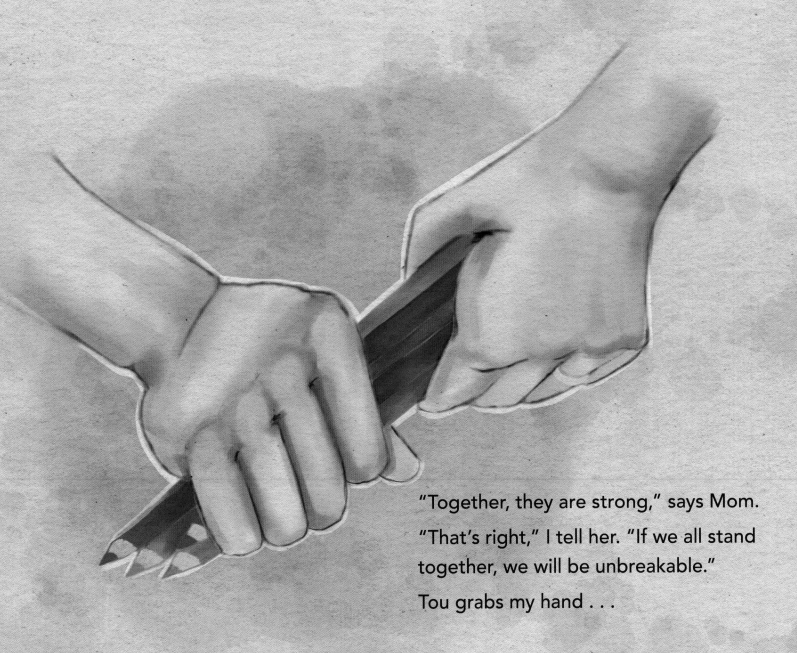

"Together, they are strong," says Mom.

"That's right," I tell her. "If we all stand together, we will be unbreakable."

Tou grabs my hand . . .

We dash out of the house and down the street.

I look back and see Mom and Dad standing at the front door, watching us.

The streets are filled with so many people, just like the time Kiara's dad took us to the fair.

"I see Kiara," Tou shouts.

"Where?"

He points: "There!"

Suddenly, I'm lifted into the air. What is Tou doing?

That's not Tou—it's Dad! He lifts me onto his shoulders.

Mom has come too, and she hands me the sign that Tou and I made.

"I wanted to keep you safe at home, Mai," she says. "But if I can't protect you from the world, I will stand by you. Now hold your sign up high."

I can see over people's heads.

Finally, I see Kiara.

Every day after school,
I have to do my homework
right away.
BUT NOT TODAY.

Today my family and I get to stand strong with my friend Kiara and her family.

AND TOGETHER, WE ARE UNBREAKABLE.

Author's Note

I was born in a refugee camp in Thailand and came to Saint Paul, Minnesota, with my family when I was just six months old. Like Mai, I am Green Hmong.

The Hmong people have a long history, but we have never had a country of our own. Long ago, the Hmong people lived in China, but in the late 1700s and into the 1800s, China used its military to suppress the Hmong and other ethnic minorities. Many Hmong people fled and settled in Laos, Vietnam, and Thailand, living mainly as farmers.

In Laos during the Vietnam War (1955–1975), the US Central Intelligence Agency recruited Hmong men, boys, and girls to fight against the Pathet Lao, a group within Laos that was working with the North Vietnamese and the Soviet Union. These groups supported a Communist government, which the US opposed, and this operation is known as the Secret War. When the Vietnam War ended and US forces left the area, the Pathet Lao began to attack the Hmong. Many Hmong people fled to refugee camps in Thailand. These refugees eventually resettled in a number of other countries, including the United States—particularly in California and Minnesota.

This history matters because it shapes the lives of Hmong children and adults today. Multiple generations experienced war, trauma, displacement, poverty, and mental health challenges. My parents had to leave their home and their way of life and come to a new country and learn a new language. In the United States, Hmong families settled into neighborhoods that are low-income, underfunded, and heavily policed. The Hmong community has a long history of struggling with the police. Due to the challenges we faced in the US, we share many similar experiences with members of the Black community. Living in the same disadvantaged areas meant that our communities were often pitted against each other when seeking resources.

It's important to recognize that the Hmong came to the US with little to no understanding of Black history or the work that Black activists had done in support of Asian American rights. We also absorbed the anti-Black racism that is prevalent throughout American society. And language is a challenge as well—there are very few resources in the Hmong language that explain Black history and the meaning behind "Black Lives Matter."

On May 25, 2020, in Minneapolis, Minnesota, a white police officer killed George Floyd, a Black father who lived in the Minneapolis area. One of the officers on the scene who watched the murder without intervening was Hmong American. In the aftermath of this event, old tensions between the Black and Hmong communities flared. I found myself in conversations that became very emotional at times as members of the older Hmong generation relived their trauma from the war and the history of tensions with the Black community. Some elders worried that speaking out would put us at risk of harm. At the same time, I saw many members of younger generations, born and raised in the US, take part in protests and stand in solidarity with the Black community.

As all this was playing out, I felt myself caught in the middle wondering, *How do we even start? How do we even navigate these conversations?* As an actor and writer, I'm a storyteller, and so I decided to write a story. I thought that perhaps a picture book about two seven-year-old girls who share a deep friendship could help make this topic easier to understand and to talk about. I was especially inspired by my younger sister, Kathy Yer Moua, who, together with her friends, attended rallies and protests in Minnesota in the aftermath of George Floyd's murder. And she, like many others, worked to educate the older Hmong generation about Black Lives Matter and the importance of speaking up.

My hope is that this book helps to bridge the generational and language gaps between the Asian and Black communities so we can stand together, in solidarity, and work together to address systemic racism and injustice.

Kathy Yer Moua (*left*) at a protest in Minneapolis in June 2020

Pronunciation Guide

Hmong: pronounced MOHNG

Kiara: pronounced key-ARE-uh; means "princess" or "first ray of sun"

Mai: pronounced MY; means "girl" or "daughter"

Tou: pronounced TO; means "son"

Words to Know

activist: a person who protests or takes other actions to bring about political or social change

Communist: someone who believes in communism or is a member of the Communist Party. Communism is a political and economic system in which key resources are owned by the public or by the state and wealth is divided among citizens equally

disadvantaged: lacking basic resources or conditions, such as safe housing and access to education and medical care, needed to achieve an equal position in society

displacement: the removal of a group of people from the place where they lived

ethnic minority: a group of people that has different national or cultural traditions from the main population in a country or region

generation: all the people born and living at about the same time; children are typically in a different generation than their parents

injustice: an act of unfair treatment; when the rights of a person or group of people are ignored or disrespected

justice: fair treatment for all people

poverty: not having enough money to meet basic needs; society is set up in such a way that people and communities experiencing poverty cannot easily get the resources they need

racism: unfair treatment against a person or group of people based on their skin color or background

rights: things all people deserve, such as freedom, education, and fair treatment

solidarity: unity of feeling or action between different people or groups of people

systemic racism: when systems of government or society are set up in a way that gives unfair treatment to groups of people based on their skin color or background

trauma: a deeply distressing or disturbing experience; it can affect a person physically and emotionally

Ways to Be an Ally

An ally is someone who supports people and communities other than their own. In this story, Mai supports Kiara and the Black community by joining a protest. There are also many ways you can be an ally at school and in your community.

Be curious about other people. Look for ways to make connections and build friendships with people who have a different background than you have. You might have friends whose skin tone is lighter or darker than yours, who speak a different language at home than you do, or who celebrate different holidays than you do.

Listen. When friends tell you about experiences they've had or something that's on their minds, listen to them. Don't tell them how they should feel or what they should think. Instead, focus on ways you can help them feel safe and supported.

Seek justice and speak up. When you notice something wrong or unfair, look for ways to make a change for the better. Find ways to work with others, whether it's classmates, your parents, or a community leader.

Be willing to apologize. We all make mistakes, and sometimes we do something that hurts a friend or classmate. When you realize you've said or done something that hurt someone else, take a deep breath. You might feel awkward or embarrassed, but know that everyone feels that way sometimes. You can apologize in person or in writing. Tell the other person you are sorry and let them know how you will do better in the future. Being an ally doesn't mean being perfect. It means doing your best, learning from your mistakes, and continuing on.

Don't give up. Sometimes change happens quickly, but often it's slow. Even though working for change can take time, know that it's still worth doing. Because when people of all different backgrounds join together, over time, they can help bring about changes that make our society more equal and more fair for everyone.

To Kathy Yer Moua —D.M.

To Reggie, Miles, Max, Olive, and Mom —K.H.

Special thanks to those who reviewed the text and layout and shared feedback, including Amy Blaubach, CEO of Curious Minds and director of Little Sprouts Academy; Nou Ly, EL teacher at Saint Paul Public Schools; Nou Moua, director of strategic initiatives and outreach at the Center for Human Rights and Global Justice at NYU School of Law; Krista Purnell, school and district success manager at Gradient Learning; Patrice Tanaka, founder and chief joy officer of Joyful Planet; and Kulap Vilaysack, founder and executive director of Laos Angeles.

Text copyright © 2022 by Doua Moua
Illustrations copyright © 2022 by Kim Holt

All rights reserved. International copyright secured. No part of this book may be reproduced, stored in a retrieval system, or transmitted in any form or by any means—electronic, mechanical, photocopying, recording, or otherwise—without the prior written permission of Lerner Publishing Group, Inc., except for the inclusion of brief quotations in an acknowledged review.

Carolrhoda Books®
An imprint of Lerner Publishing Group, Inc.
241 First Avenue North
Minneapolis, MN 55401 USA

For reading levels and more information, look up this title at www.lernerbooks.com.

Designed by Emily Harris.
Main body text set in Avenir LT Pro. Typeface provided by Linotype AG.
The illustrations in this book were created with digital paint.

Library of Congress Cataloging-in-Publication Data

Names: Moua, Doua, 1987– author. | Holt, Kim (Kim T.), illustrator.
Title: Today is different / Doua Moua ; illustrated by Kim Holt.
Description: Minneapolis : Carolrhoda Books, [2022] | Audience: Ages 5–9 | Audience: Grades 2–3 | Summary: "Two girls—one Hmong American and one Black—stand together in solidarity with their communities to protest systemic racism and injustice" —Provided by publisher.
Identifiers: LCCN 2021024037 (print) | LCCN 2021024038 (ebook) | ISBN 9781728430294 (library binding) | ISBN 9781728443904 (ebook)
Subjects: CYAC: Hmong Americans—Fiction. | African Americans—Fiction. | Protest movements—Fiction. | Justice—Fiction.
Classification: LCC PZ7.1.M679 To 2022 (print) | LCC PZ7.1.M679 (ebook) | DDC [E]—dc23

LC record available at https://lccn.loc.gov/2021024037
LC ebook record available at https://lccn.loc.gov/2021024038

Manufactured in the United States of America
1-49473-49526-8/4/2021